www.mascotbooks.com

Count On™ Arizona®: Fun Facts from 1 to 12

For more information, please contact:
Mascot Books
560 Herndon Parkway #120
Herndon, VA 20170
info@mascotbooks.com

CPSIA Code: PRT0716A
ISBN-13: 978-1-63177-528-4

Printed in the United States

COUNT ON ™

Fun Facts from 1 to 12

by Robin A. Ward, Ph.D.

UA is **one** mile from downtown Tucson,
nestled in a desert habitat.

2

Our **two** mascots are Wilma and Wilbur.
They are the cutest Wildcats!

Three colors adorn A mountain:
red, white, and blue.

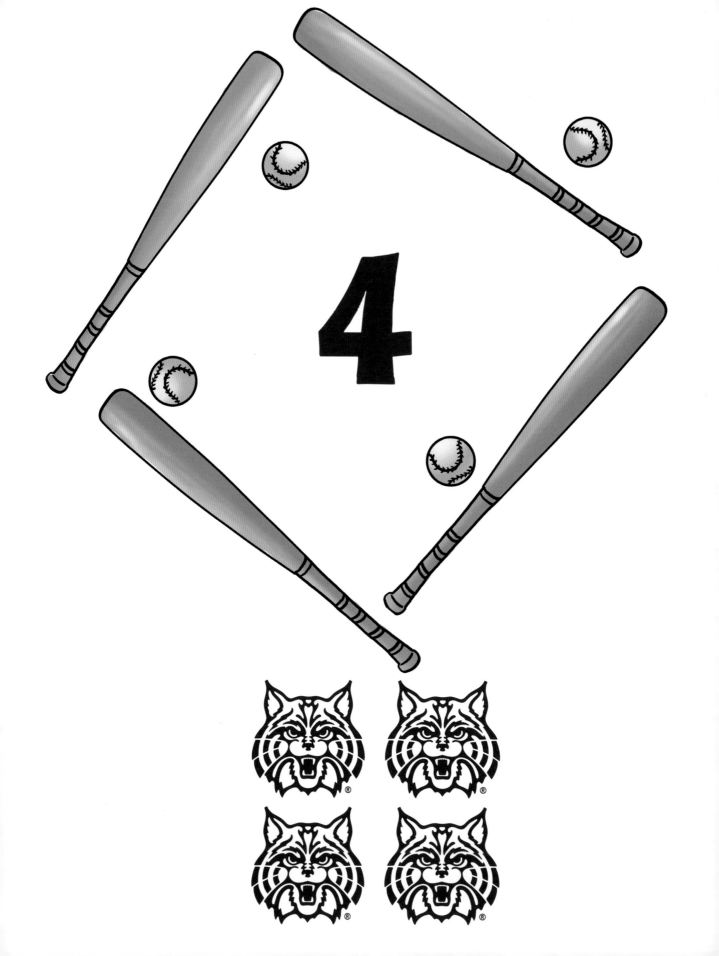

We've won **four** national championships in baseball and have more in our field of view.

The **Five** Cs are a part of our state's history: cattle, copper, citrus, climate, and cotton.

6

Six is the number of faculty when Old Main opened its classrooms in 1891.

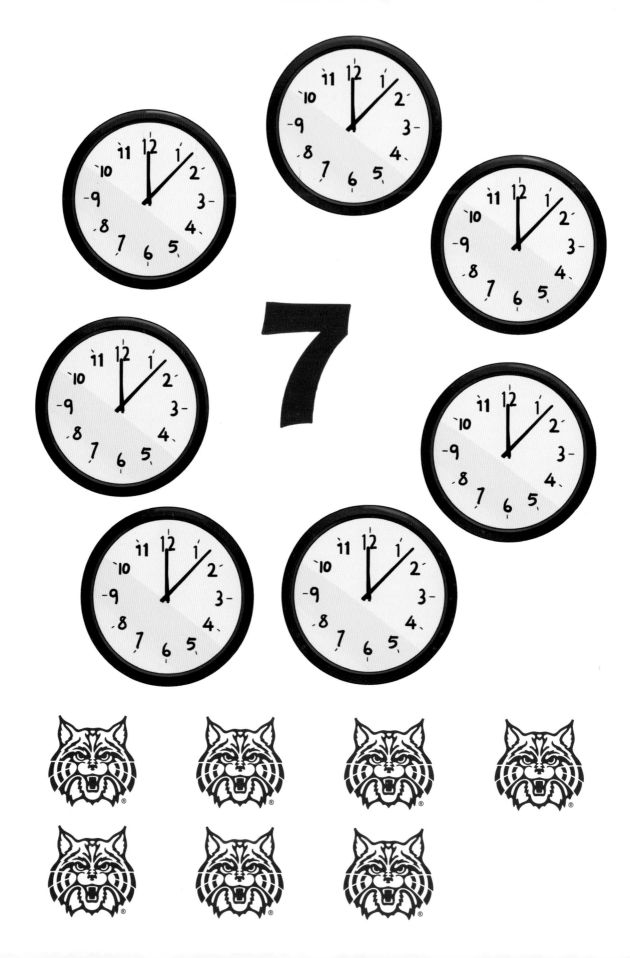

The U.S.S. Arizona's bell is rung **seven** times on the third Wednesday of every month.

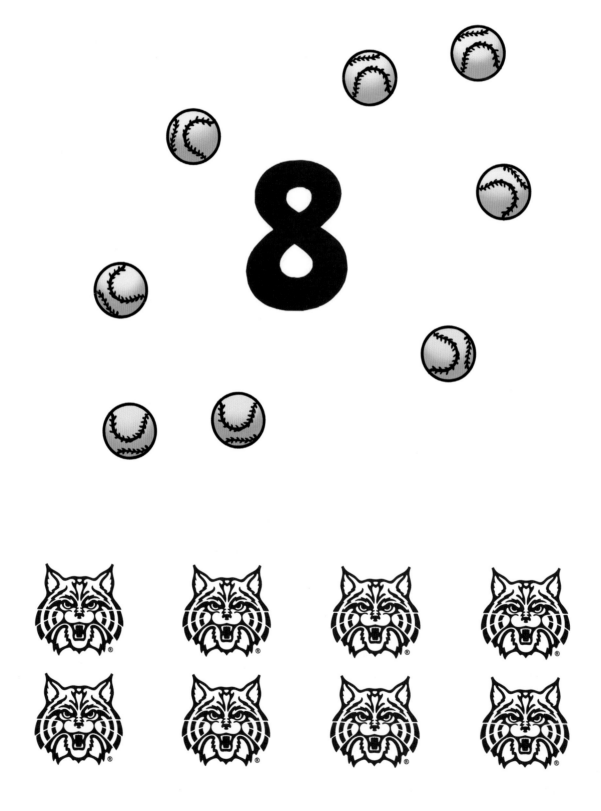

Our women's softball team has won
eight College World Series titles.
Coach Candrea will win more. We have a hunch!

The Eller College of Management offers
nine business majors,
launching the careers of many alum,
both women and men.

UA has retired lots of jerseys,
like basketball's Mike Bibby's number **ten**.

UA's **eleven**th head basketball coach was Lute Olson, who was inducted into the 2002 Basketball Hall of Fame.

12

Our conference is the Pac **12**.
We strive to win all of our games!

I wish we could keep counting!

But instead, I just have to say:

If you ever want to count again,

why not count on **UA**!

A Note to Parents

Notice that the even numbers in this book appear in blue and the odd numbers in red. This should not come as a surprise, as the word blue contains 4 letters (an even number) and red contains 3 letters (an odd number).

Guide your reader to discover that even numbers can be grouped into pairs, indicated by the wildcats placed vertically two-by-two on each left-hand page. You cannot create pairs with an odd number of objects, as you will always have one odd man (I mean, wildcat) out!

On each left-hand page, notice that the number of images around each numeral represents that number as well.

Why count to 12 instead of stopping at 10? Because UA is now in the Pac 12!

Go Wildcats!

Enjoy coloring our mascots, Wilbur and Wilma.

About the Author

Robin and her husband, Chris DelConte, both worked at the University of Arizona from 2000 to 2006, Robin as a Professor of Mathematics Education, and Chris as a Senior Associate Athletics Director. Robin is now a Professor of Mathematics at Rice University in Houston, Texas, and her husband is the Director of Athletics at TCU. Robin and Chris are both very fond of Tucson as their two daughters, Sienna and Sophia, were born at the University of Arizona Medical Center.

Robin's career includes working as an aerospace engineer and a NASA educational consultant, and her extensive research has been published nationally and internationally. She is the author of five teacher resource books on using the visual arts and children's literature in the K-8 mathematics classroom. She is regularly heard encouraging teachers and students to put on their *math goggles®* as a way to see math in art and in their world.

Robin is the author of *Count on TCU: Fun Facts from 1 to 12* and *Count on Rice: Fun Facts from 1 to 12.*

Robin's ultimate personal goal is for all students to fall in love with mathematics.

So, let's begin by counting...*Count on Arizona!*

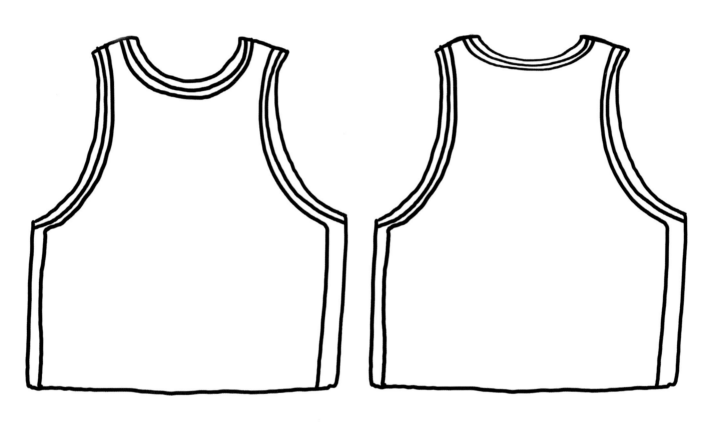

If you were an Arizona Wildcat, what sport would you play?
Design the front and back of your own jersey!